I0782088

DYING for Recipes

The Secret Recipes of Eleanor Penrose

An unauthorized cookbook
by

Patricia Brown

GladEye Press
www.gladeyepress.com

Springfield, OR

In the Beginning …

It didn't start all at once, the deep abiding friendship, the sharing of gains and losses, dreams and nightmares, the trust and confidences, joys and sorrows, all nurtured over hundreds of meetings during sips of coffee and bites of toast.

It's what every person hungers for but rarely finds—enduring relationships with those who somehow turn out to be soul sisters, bosom buddies, and kindred spirits. Friends who tell you the truth when you need to hear it, don't judge you when you make a mess of things, and love you just because they see who you are.

That's how it was with our coffee group. Pearl introduced us all. She was the social link. Josephine provided the common sense that kept us on an even keel, while Cleo added the wild and crazy ideas that often led us into trouble but sometimes to the solutions we needed. Dede was the fountain of information about all things, people, and places. Her mind was a steel trap, holding the history and traditions of the world in which we lived. I was new to the group and like to think I also contributed something. I could research and organize, but snooping was my specialty. We could all cook.

After years of sharing gossip, secrets, and recipes, we began to delve into mysteries. Maybe it was because we were growing older too that we noticed a series of elder deaths and set out to discover if they were murders. (*A Recipe for Dying*)

Once we got into snooping there was no going back. I began a relationship with Angus, a retired homicide detective, and the coffee group once again became involved in a twisted tale of murder and deception. (*Dying for Diamonds*)

Then a body washed up on the beach and we discovered unsavory and dangerous people living among us in our sleepy little town of Waterton. Who would have guessed what was going on? (*Under a Dying Moon*)

Even small towns have their bullies, but we never would have thought some of our so-called pillars of the community might have the kind of secrets we uncovered. Some people will do anything to stay on top … but murder? (*Dying to Win*)

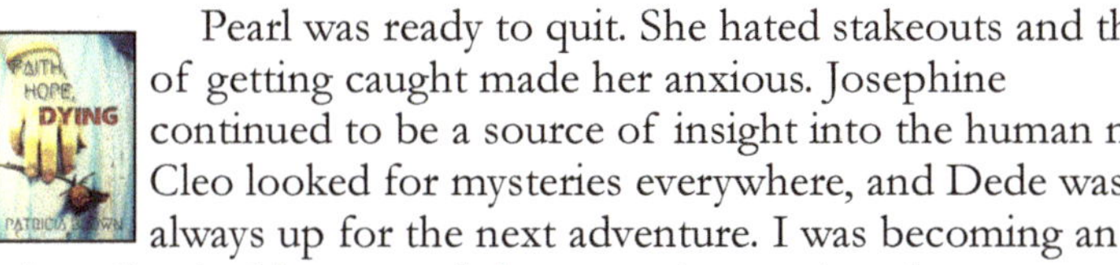

Pearl was ready to quit. She hated stakeouts and the fear of getting caught made her anxious. Josephine continued to be a source of insight into the human mind. Cleo looked for mysteries everywhere, and Dede was always up for the next adventure. I was becoming an adrenaline junkie, too and the mysteries continued to come our way when Angus brought home a dog who helped dig up a cold case. (*Faith, Hope, Dying*)

Who knows what will happen next while we wait for another mystery, and I'm sure there will be one. We might as well enjoy ourselves. I think I'll plan a party.

—*Eleanor Penrose*

It never occurred to me that someone would want to steal my collection of recipes. People have often asked for them and I have shared a few … well, maybe one or two … okay, one, but who can blame me when I have a reputation as a food magician? Everyone knows that magicians never give away their secrets.

That's why it puzzled me when I attended a barbeque at an aquaintance's house and was served marinated pork chops, which suspiciously tasted exactly like the ones I make. They were quite delicious and I enjoyed them very much. I suppose it's possible that they could have discovered a similar recipe somewhere …

 # Marinated Pork Chops

Ingredients

Marinade

1 cup hoisin sauce
1 tablespoon sugar
1 ½ tablespoons tamari soy sauce
1 ½ tablespoons sherry vinegar
1 ½ tablespoons rice vinegar
1 scallion, white and two-thirds green, minced
1 teaspoon Tabasco sauce
1 ½ teaspoons Lee Kum Kee black bean chile sauce
1 ½ teaspoons peeled and grated fresh ginger
1 ½ tablespoons minced garlic
¾ teaspoon freshly ground white pepper
¼ cup fresh cilantro leaves and stems, minced
1 tablespoon sesame oil

Directions

Have your butcher thin cut 12 pork chops and trim the excess meat and fat away from the ends, leaving the bones exposed. Combine the marinade ingredients and add the pork chops, coating them liberally. Marinate for at least 3 hours in the refrigerator.

Grill the chops for 5 minutes on each side, basting with the marinade at a low temperature, making sure not to char the meat.

Chops are ready when a temperature of 139° is reached.

Serve with green beans and mashed potatoes. Pair with a pinot noir.

I usually keep my special recipes in a notebook alongside many cookbooks stored on my kitchen bookshelves. (Nothing is as clever as hiding something in plain sight.) However; when I sought out a recipe for fish stew, the notebook was missing. Something fishy was definitely going on.

Yummy Jelly

Blob the jellyfish swims through the sea

Filled with delicious yummy jelly

Blob the jellyfish ate the jelly

That felt so good in his round belly

Blob the jellyfish laid down for a nap

And dreamt of jelly sitting in his lap

Yummy yummy yummy jelly

—Maggie Mulder

Bouillabaisse with a Rouille

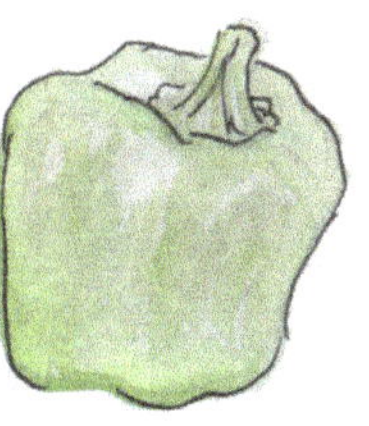

Ingredients

Rouille

⅔ cup chopped bottled roasted red bell peppers
3 tablespoons reduced-fat mayonnaise
Add ¼ teaspoon ground red pepper for extra spice

Bouillabaisse

1 tablespoon olive oil
1 cup chopped onion
2 garlic cloves, minced
¾ cup chopped plum tomato
½ teaspoon saffron threads, lightly crushed

3 ½ cups cubed red potato
2 ½ cups thinly sliced fennel bulb
3 cups clam juice
1 (14-oz.) can fat-free, less-sodium chicken broth
24 littleneck clams
24 mussels, scrubbed and debearded
12 ounces large shrimp, peeled and deveined
1 pound white fish filet, cut into 12 (2-inch) pieces
6 tablespoons chopped fresh parsley

Directions

Preheat oven to 400°.

Prepare rouille by combining the roasted red bell peppers and mayonnaise in a blender or food processor until smooth and set aside.

To make bouillabaisse, first heat oil in a large Dutch oven over medium heat. Then add onion and garlic and cook 8 minutes until tender. Add tomato and cook 3 minutes. Add saffron and cook 30 seconds. Next add potato, fennel, clam juice, and broth and bring to a boil. Reduce heat, cover and simmer 3 minutes. Then add shrimp and fish, cover and simmer 5 minutes until shells open, shrimp is done, and fish flakes easily with a fork.

Discard unopened shells. Serve with lots of crusty bread and rouille. Pair with sauvignon blanc or gewürztraminer.

My mind shifted into overdrive. Who had been in my house and had access to my kitchen and those recipes? Should I even suspect my friends or family? It never occurred to me that someone close to me would be so ruthless as to steal from me. If they wanted a recipe, surely all they needed to do was ask. It had to be someone else. Perhaps there had been a break-in. I began searching in earnest for clues.

Beef Wellington

Ingredients

1 (2 lb.) center-cut beef tenderloin, trimmed
Kosher salt
Freshly ground black pepper
Oil olive, for greasing
2 tablespoons Dijon mustard
1 ½ lb. mixed mushrooms roughly chopped
1 shallot, roughly chopped
Leaves from 1 thyme sprig
2 tablespoons unsalted butter
12 thin slices prosciutto
Flour for dusting
14 oz. frozen puff pastry, thawed
1 large egg, beaten
Flaky salt, for sprinkling

Directions

Tie tenderloin in 4 places using kitchen twine and season with salt and pepper.

Coat bottom of a heavy skillet with olive oil over high heat. Sear tenderloin until well-browned on all sides for about 2 minutes on each side including the ends. Set aside on a plate to cool, then cut off twine and coat with mustard. Place in refrigerator.

Pulse mushrooms, shallots, and thyme in a food processor until finely chopped to make the duxelles.

Add butter and melt over medium heat in the skillet. Add mushroom mix and cook about 25 minutes until liquid has evaporated. Season with salt and pepper and cool in refrigerator.

Lay plastic wrap on counter, overlapping it so that it is twice the length and width of the tenderloin. Overlap the prosciutto on the plastic wrap into a rectangle that is big enough to cover the whole tenderloin. Then evenly spread the duxelles thinly over the prosciutto.

Season the tenderloin and place it at the bottom of the prosciutto, rolling the meat into prosciutto-mushroom mixture using the plastic wrap to get a tight roll. Tuck prosciutto ends as you roll twisting the ends of plastic wrap tightly and chill in the refrigerator to help maintain its shape.

Heat the oven to 425°. Flour the counter lightly, spread out puff pastry and roll it into a rectangle that will cover the tenderloin. Remove tenderloin from plastic wrap and put it on the bottom of the puff pastry. Brush the remaining edges with egg wash and tightly roll the beef into the pastry.

Trim extra pastry and crimp edges with a fork to seal the covered log. Wrap the roll tightly in plastic and chill for 20 minutes.

Remove plastic and transfer the roll to a foil-lined baking sheet. Brush it with egg wash and sprinkle with flaky salt.

Bake until the pastry is golden and the center registers 120 degrees F. for medium rare (approximately 40 to 45 minutes). Let rest 10 minutes before carving and serve.

Pair with a cabernet sauvignon or merlot.

My sister always wanted to know the ingredients for a salad I routinely brought to family gatherings, but I repeatedly ignored her requests. She began calling it "Salad X." I know she would definitely snoop to find this recipe, but she lives in California and hasn't been in my house for ages. Then there was a man named Peter who asked for it at a house party my daughter hosted. I've seen him several times since, but he's never been in my home either.

Salad X

Ingredients

3 cups cauliflower chopped
3 cups broccoli chopped
2 stalks celery diced
½ cup sweet or red onion diced
⅓ cup roasted cashews chopped
¾ cup frozen peas
Fresh dill to taste

Dressing

Combine the following ingredients: mayo, lemon juice, salt, and small amount of sugar and add to vegetables.

Cleo raved about this recipe for beef stew. I know she is a horrible snoop and quite capable of stealing my recipe, but she would never take the time to prepare most of my dishes.

Beef Bourguignon

Ingredients

3 pounds beef chuck or other boneless stewing beef, cut into 2-inch cubes and patted dry
2 ¼ teaspoons kosher salt, more to taste
½ teaspoon freshly ground black pepper
5 ounces lardons, pancetta or bacon, diced (about 1¼ cups)
1 onion, finely chopped
1 large carrot, sliced
2 garlic cloves, minced
1 teaspoon tomato paste
2 tablespoons all-purpose flour
1 750-milliliter bottle of red wine
1 large bay leaf
1 large sprig of thyme
8 ounces pearl onions, peeled (12 to 15)
8 ounces cremini mushrooms, halved if large (about 4 cups)
1 tablespoon extra-virgin olive oil
Pinch of sugar

Directions

Season meat with 2 teaspoons of salt and ½ teaspoon pepper and set aside at room temperature for at least 30 minutes.

Cook lardons over medium-low heat in a heavy Dutch oven with a tight-fitting lid until the lardons are brown and crisp. Then transfer them to a paper towel with a slotted spoon leaving the fat in the pan.

Heat oven to 350°. Heat pot to medium-high and lay half the beef cubes in a single layer in the pan, leaving space between pieces. Brown well on all sides, transfer to a plate and repeat with the remaining meat.

Reduce heat, stir in onion, carrot and ¼ teaspoon salt and cook about 10 minutes. (Add potatoes here if Angus is coming to dinner. He prefers the small Yukon golds.) Stir.

Add garlic and tomato paste and cook for 1 minute. Stir in flour, cook for 1 minute and add wine, bay leaf, and thyme, scraping up the brown bits at the bottom. Add the beef and half the lardons back to the pot, cover, and bake in the oven for about 1½ hours turning meat midway.

Combine the pearl onions, mushrooms, ¼ cup water, the olive oil and a pinch of salt, pepper and sugar in a large skillet over high heat while the meat is cooking. Bring to a simmer, cover and reduce heat to medium for 15 minutes. Uncover and brown the vegetables over high heat for 5 to 7 minutes tossing frequently.

Scatter onions and mushrooms along with the remaining lardons over the stew, top with parsley and serve with crusty bread for mopping. Pair with a red burgundy wine.

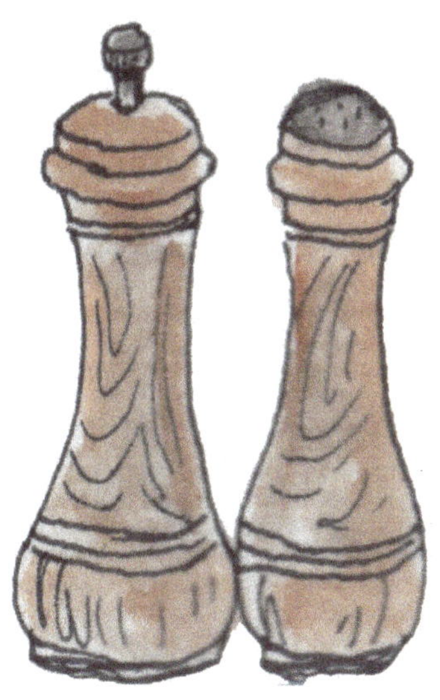

Tex-Mex Skillet (Feathers' favorite vegan dinner)

I never fed Feathers, my beloved African gray parrot anything like this! The results would be a disaster of a magnitude that I can only imagine.

Ingredients

3 cups uncooked whole wheat macaroni or pasta spirals
1 medium onion diced
1 tablespoon olive oil or water for sautéing
2 cups ground gluten or vegeburger (soy curls work if you have a gluten intolerance)
1 4.5 oz. can of diced green chilies
2 14.5 oz. cans stewed tomatoes Mexican style (I use a can of stewed tomatoes or about 1 ½ cups Salsa works as well)
1 15 oz. can (or 2 cups home-cooked pinto beans) drained but not rinsed
2 tablespoons vegetarian Worchestershire sauce
½ cup Vegenaise or cashew mayonnaise
1 cup whole kernel corn
1 cup crushed tortilla chips (optional)
Hot sauce can be added if you like it hotter.

Directions

Cook macaroni and set aside. Using a large skillet, saute onions in oil or water until clear. Add all the other ingredients and stir well. (Leave the chips out for later). Then stir in the macaroni. Serve in a bowl with the tortilla chips on top.

This can also be placed in a casserole dish with tortilla chips on top and baked at 350° until bubbly.

Add the following cheese sauce to the casserole before adding the chips and baking.

Pimiento Cheese Sauce

Ingredients

1 cup water
1 ¼ teaspoons salt
6 tablespoons raw cashew pieces
2 teaspoons onion powder
1 tablespoon tahini (sesame seed paste)

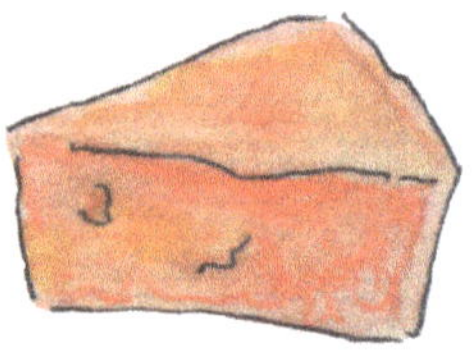

¼ teaspoon garlic powder
3 tablespoons Red Star nutritional yeast
2 tablespoons fresh lemon juice

Directions

In a blender, combine all the ingredients and blend on high until smooth and creamy (1 to 2 minutes). Transfer to a bowl, cover and refrigerate until time to add to the dish.

Pearl has no need to steal any of my recipes and she is always extremely generous with her own. It almost makes me feel guilty that I refused to give her the ingredients I used in my easy Swiss steak dish.

Pearl's Walnut Walkaways

Ingredients

1 envelope active dry yeast
1 teaspoon sugar
¼ cup warm water
flour and butter:
2 cups flour
¼ teaspoon salt
¾ cup (1 ¼ sticks) butter
1 egg

Filling

3-ounces cream cheese, softened
½ cup sugar
1 tablespoon orange zest
1 teaspoon fresh orange juice
2 tablespoons fresh lemon juice
½ cup finely chopped walnuts
Frosting:
1 cup confectioner sugar
1 tablespoon melted butter
1 tablespoon milk
½ teaspoon vanilla

Directions

Lightly grease a cookie sheet and set aside. Preheat oven to 375°.

Chop the walnuts and set aside.

Add yeast, sugar, and warm water to a work bowl. Let the yeast stand for 5 to 10 minutes, until it becomes foamy.

In a medium-sized bowl combine flour and salt.

Cut the butter into the flour until crumbly.

Add the butter and flour mixture to the work bowl containing the yeast.

Add the egg to the work bowl.

Mix the yeast, flour, and egg mixture on medium speed until it makes a soft dough. (If you are using a stand mixer, use a regular paddle beater, not the dough hook.)

Split the dough into two rounds.

On a lightly floured surface, roll out each dough round into a 13 × 9 rectangle.

In a medium-sized bowl, beat cream cheese, sugar, orange zest, orange juice, and lemon juice until well-blended and light.

Spread the cream cheese mixture over each rectangle of dough; leaving a half-inch edge.

Sprinkle chopped walnuts over the filling.

Beginning on the long (13-inch) side, roll the dough tightly.

Pinch the ends together and tuck under.

Place roll seam side down on the greased cookie sheet. Each roll will spread out while baking so allow 2 inches of space around the outside edge of the cookie sheet and 2 to 3 inches in between the two rolls.

Take a paring knife and make a shallow lengthwise score down the center of each roll.

Bake for 20 to 25 minutes or until the roll has spread out and is a light golden color.

Cool and drizzle with frosting.

Cut and serve.

Dede is a wonderful cook and never hesitates to give her recipes away. However, I suspect she doesn't always share all the details that make her desserts so delicious. In fact, I suspect she doubles the filling in her Lemon Angel Pie.

Dede's Lemon Angel Pie

Ingredients

1 cup sugar
4 eggs separated, room temperature
¼ teaspoon cream of tartar
½ cup sugar
3 tablespoons lemon juice
1 tablespoon grated lemon rind
¼ teaspoon salt
2 cups whipping cream

Directions

Beat egg whites until white and fluffy. Add in sugar gradually and cream of tartar. Beat until stiff but not dry (it's ok if this doesn't happen).

Pour into a buttered 9" deep dish glass pie dish and press up against the sides

Bake meringue crust at 300° for 45–60 minutes. Cool.

Filling

Take 4 egg yolks and beat slightly.

Stir in ½ cup sugar, 3 tablespoons lemon juice and 1 tablespoon grated lemon rind, ¼ teaspoon salt.

Cook until thickened in microwave for 4 minutes (stir every 30 seconds). Cool.

Whip 2 cups whipping cream and fold ½ of whip cream into lemon mixture.

Pour into cooled meringue shell. Top with the remaining whip cream. Chill for 24 hours.

(This is a delicious pie, but it was much higher when Dede made it.)

Always concerned about her image, Dede seems perfectly pure and innocent, but I know she has a naughty side and there is absolute proof of it in her candlestick salad. Could she be the thief?

Dede's Candlestick Salad

Ingredients

Bananas
Lettuce
Pineapple rings
Whipped cream
Maraschino cherries

Use the lettuce leaves to create a bed for the Candle Salad to sit on. The lettuce is more for decoration than eating, so feel free to use the tougher outer leaves from the head of the lettuce. Just give the leaves a good rinse and pat them dry before using.

Place a pineapple ring or two in the middle of the bed of lettuce.

Cut the banana in half (not lengthwise) and place it in the middle of the pineapple ring. If you are having trouble keeping the banana half from tipping over, try adding a little whipped cream, ~~cottage cheese~~ or cream cheese to the cut side of the banana to help it stay put. Some people may use whipped cream on the side of the banana to simulate dripping wax. (gross)

Poke a toothpick on the top of the banana and stick a maraschino onto it. Make sure you tell people about the toothpick to avoid any unwanted injuries.

Dede swears this recipe appeared in her mother's church cookbook. I sincerely doubt their thoughts were any purer than ours.

I find it suspicious that cottage cheese has been crossed out. It makes me think that my publisher may somehow be involved since he once proclaimed he could not possibly like anyone who ate cottage cheese.

Nikki's Oatmeal Cranberry Cookies

Makes about 4 dozen cookies.

¾ Cup butter, softened
¾ cup firmly packed brown sugar
½ cup granulated sugar
2 eggs
1 teaspoon vanilla
1 ½ cups all-purpose flour
1 teaspoon baking soda
1 teaspoon cinnamon
½ teaspoon salt
3 cups oats
1 cup dried cranberries
1 cup semisweet chocolate chips

Directions

Preheat oven to 350°.

In a large bowl, beat butter and sugars on medium speed of electric mixer until creamy.

Add eggs (one at a time) and vanilla; beat well.

Add combined flour, baking soda, cinnamon and salt; mix well. Add oats, cranberries, and chocolate chips; mix well.

Drop dough by rounded tablespoonfuls onto ungreased cookie sheets.

Bake 8 to 10 minutes or until light golden brown. Cool 1 minute on cookie sheets; remove to wire rack. Cool completely. Store tightly covered.

The apple jumped out of the pie.

The apple jumped out of the pie.

The apple jumped out of the pie,

Cause he didn't want to die

In the oven!

—Sung by Emmy Mulder, Age 5

Apple Pie

Ingredients for filling

6 cups Granny Smith apples peeled, cored and cubed or sliced
1 cup sugar
2 tablespoons Minute tapioca
½ teaspoon ground cinnamon
¼ teaspoon ground nutmeg

Directions

Mix all filling ingredients together in a bowl and let sit for 15 minutes.

Gramma O's No Fail Pie Crust

Ingredients

3 cups all-purpose flour
1 ¼ cup butter (cut very cold butter into small cubes)
1 teaspoon salt
1 egg, well-beaten
5 tablespoons water (icy cold)
1 tablespoon vinegar

Directions

Put flour, butter, and salt in food processor and pulse until mixed.

Combine egg, water, and vinegar and pour into flour mixture all at once. Pulse just until flour is all moistened. Divide into fourths and roll out on a lightly floured surface.

Line a pie plate with pie crust and add the apple filling.

Dot with a tablespoon of butter, cover with top crust, seal and flute. Cut several slits in the top crust.

Bake in a preheated 400° oven for 45–50 minutes or until juices form and bubble.

Cool and serve with vanilla and salted caramel ice cream. Serves 8, or 1 if Angus is over for dinner.

The real secret ingredient is chemistry. Temperature is the key. I'm positive this is the most wanted recipe. Everyone I know would kill for this delicate pie crust.

Angus is not a big fan of pasta. He would rather eat meat and potatoes, but he did indicate an interest in bacon and eggs in this carbonara recipe. Certainly, my gentleman friend cannot be a suspect, although he watches carefully when we are in the kitchen together.

Pasta Carbonara

4 to 6 servings

Note: This recipe uses raw eggs, which are basically cooked by tossing with hot pasta. They are cooked just enough to thicken the eggs into a sauce. The garlic is optional. "Guanciale," or pork jowl, is traditionally used in this dish, so if you can get it, by all means use it.

Ingredients

1 tablespoon extra virgin olive oil or unsalted butter
½ pound pancetta or thick cut bacon, diced
1 to 2 garlic cloves, minced, about 1 teaspoon (optional)
3 to 4 whole eggs
1 cup grated Parmesan or pecorino cheese
1 pound spaghetti (or bucatini or fettuccine)
Kosher salt and freshly ground black pepper to taste

Directions

Heat the pasta water: Put a large pot of salted water on to boil (1 tablespoon salt for every 2 quarts of water.)

While the water is coming to a boil, heat the olive oil or butter in a large sauté pan over medium heat. Add the bacon or pancetta and cook slowly until crispy.

Add the garlic (if using) and cook another minute, then turn off the heat and put the pancetta and garlic into a large bowl.

In a small bowl, beat the eggs and mix in about half of the cheese.

Once the water has reached a rolling boil, add the dry pasta, and cook, uncovered, at a rolling boil until done.

When the pasta is al dente (still a little firm, not mushy), use tongs to move it to the bowl with the bacon and garlic. Let it be dripping wet. Reserve some of the pasta water.

Move the pasta from the pot to the bowl quickly, as you want the pasta to be hot. It's the heat of the pasta that will heat the eggs sufficiently to create a creamy sauce.

Toss everything to combine, allowing the pasta to cool just enough so that it doesn't make the eggs curdle when you mix them in. (That's the tricky part.)

Serve at once with the rest of the parmesan and freshly ground black pepper. If you want, sprinkle with a little fresh chopped parsley. Pair with Frascati or pinot bianco.

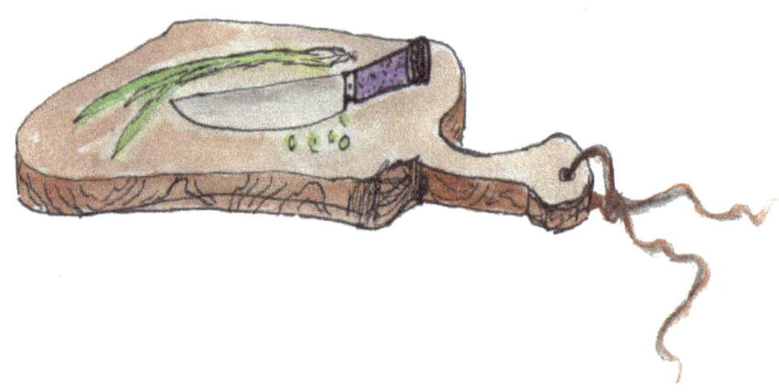

I have searched the house carefully for evidence that someone broke in but have so far found nothing. Perhaps I should ask Angus to check as well. He may find a clue that I missed. I'm sure he can be trusted. In return, I think I'll make him something delectable.

Steak and Potatoes with Balsamic Cranberry Pan Sauce

Ingredients

1 yellow onion
¼ oz. rosemary
16 oz. Yukon potatoes
4 oz. red cabbage
1 teaspoon mustard seeds
2 tablespoons white wine vinegar
12 oz. sirloin steak
½ tablespoon balsamic vinegar
1 ½ tablespoon soy sauce
4 teaspoons cranberry jam

Directions

Preheat oven to 425°.

Wash and dry all produce. Halve, peel, and thinly slice onion and cabbage. Strip rosemary leaves discarding stems and finely chop until you have 1 tablespoon.

Halve potatoes lengthwise and cut into 1-inch-thick wedges (like steak fries). Toss potatoes on a baking sheet with a large drizzle of olive oil, chopped rosemary and salt and pepper. (I prefer to use Johnny's Seasoning Salt). Roast until lightly browned and crisp, about 30–35 minutes.

Heat a large drizzle of oil in a medium pan on medium-high heat. Add onion and cabbage and cook until softened, about 5 minutes, tossing throughout.

Add mustard seeds and cook until they start to pop. Stir in white wine vinegar, sugar, and a pinch of salt.

Reduce heat to low, cover, and cook until cabbage is tender, about 10 minutes.

While cabbage cooks, heat a drizzle of oil in another medium pan over medium-high heat. Pat steak dry with a paper towel, then season all over with salt and pepper. Add to pan and sear until browned and cooked to desired doneness, 4–7 minutes per side. Remove and set aside to rest.

Add ½ tablespoons balsamic vinegar, 1½ tablespoons soy sauce, cranberry jam, and 3 tablespoons water to same pan over medium heat. Stir to combine. Let simmer until reduced to a syrupy consistency, about 2–3 minutes. Remove from heat.

Thinly slice steak against the grain. Divide steak, potatoes, and cabbage between plates. Drizzle glaze over steak and serve. Pair with a Sangiovese.

Tuna Noodle Casserole

Yield: About 4 servings

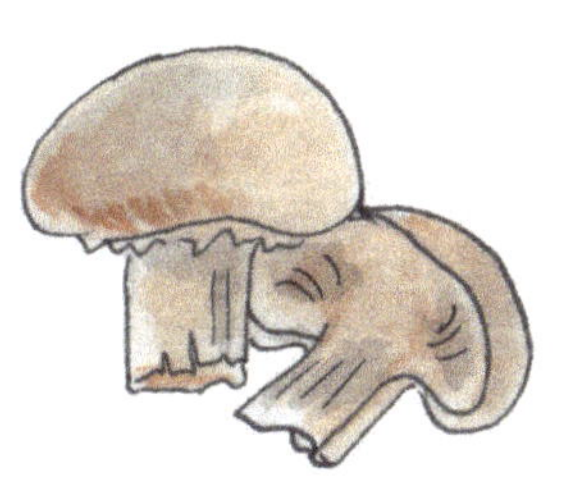

Ingredients

2 cups uncooked egg noodles
¼ cup unsalted butter, divided
½ cup minced onion
¼ cup minced celery
8 oz. fresh mushrooms, sliced, optional
¼ cup all-purpose flour
2 ½ cups whole milk
1 teaspoon salt, or to taste
¼ teaspoon freshly cracked black pepper
¼ teaspoon Old Bay seasoning
¼ teaspoon Cajun or Creole seasoning, or to taste, optional
1 cup frozen peas, thawed
1 (12 ounce) can chunk tuna (preferably in oil), well drained
1 cup crushed kettle style potato chips, French fried onions, or
fresh buttered bread crumbs

Directions

Preheat oven to 350°. Butter a 2-quart casserole dish; set aside.
Cook the noodles al dente, about 1 minute less than the package
directions, drain and set aside.

Meanwhile, in a large skillet, melt 2 tablespoons of the butter. Add
onion and celery and fresh mushrooms, if using, cooking until
softened, about 3 minutes. Add remaining butter, sprinkle in the
flour and continue cooking and stirring for about 2 minutes. Slowly
begin adding 2 cups of the milk. Add the seasonings and peas and
toss to coat, then add the tuna and noodles; mix. If mixture is too
dry, stir in additional milk as needed to moisten. Taste and adjust
seasonings; turn out into the buttered casserole dish.

Sprinkle topping over casserole. Bake uncovered at 350° for about
20–25 minutes, or until bubbly and heated through.

Double for a 4 quart (9 × 13) casserole dish. Stir in ½ cup shredded cheese with the tuna and noodles, if desired. May substitute
drained, canned mushrooms for the fresh; add with the tuna and
noodles. May also substitute frozen mixed vegetables, thawed, for
the peas. Pair with a chardonnay.

Potatoes au Gratin

Ingredients

1 thinly sliced yellow onion
1 tablespoon butter (unsalted) plus some for greasing the pan
2 tablespoons olive oil
2 pounds peeled potatoes
2 ½ cups heavy cream, divided
2 cups Gruyère cheese or any grated cheese that melts easily (Angus likes cheddar)
Salt and pepper, to taste

Directions

Preheat the oven to 350°. Grease a baking dish with butter.

Heat a medium pan and add the butter and olive oil. Add the onions and cook until tender, about 10 minutes, on medium-low heat. Put aside.

Thinly slice the potatoes. Add 2 cups of cream, the sliced potatoes, salt, and pepper to a large saucepan. Turn the heat to medium, and bring the mixture to a boil. Keep the potatoes simmering for about 10 minutes.

Arrange the potatoes in the prepared baking dish with the cream mixture. Top them with onions. Pour the remaining ½ cup of heavy cream over the potato mixture. Sprinkle the grated Gruyère or cheddar cheese evenly on top.

Bake for 1–1 ¾ hours. At this point, the potatoes should be very soft, the top should be golden brown, and the sauce should be bubbling. Remove from the oven and let the dish cool for 10 minutes.

Swiss Steak

Ingredients

2 pounds bottom round roast (Cut into ½ in. thick slices or have your butcher cube the steaks for you)
1 teaspoon salt (or to taste)
1 teaspoon pepper (or to taste)
½ cup flour (all-purpose)
3 tablespoons olive oil
1 onion (sliced)
4 cloves garlic (minced)
1 tablespoon tomato paste
14.5 oz. diced fire-roasted tomatoes (1 can)
2 cups beef broth (low sodium)
2 teaspoons Italian seasoning
1 tablespoon Worcestershire sauce
1 tablespoon parsley (freshly chopped)

Directions

Swiss the steak. Use a meat tenderizer mallet to poke holes into each slice of steak on both sides (Cubed steaks are readily available and allow skipping this step.)

Dredge through flour. Generously salt the beef slices with salt and pepper. Add the flour to a shallow bowl. Dredge each piece of beef well in the flour.

Sear the steak. Heat 2 tablespoons of the olive oil in large, deep skillet over medium-high heat (I like to use my 6 quart Dutch oven). Add the dredged beef to the skillet and cook for 4–5 minutes per side, or until seared and well browned. Remove the beef from the skillet and set aside.

Sauté onion: Add the remaining tablespoon of olive oil to the skillet along with the onions. Cook for 3–4 minutes, until they soften and become translucent. Add the garlic and cook for 30 seconds or until aromatic.

Add the rest of ingredients: Stir in the tomato paste and cook for 1 minute, then add the diced tomatoes, broth, Italian seasoning, and Worcestershire sauce. Stir everything together well.

Braise. Bring the mixture to a boil, then reduce the heat to a simmer. Add the beef back to the skillet and make sure it's fully submerged. Cover and cook for 1½ hours, or until the sauce has reduced to your liking and the beef is tender. Stir occasionally. Setting the oven for 350° and putting the Dutch oven in for the required time frees the hostess to mingle with her guests.

Finish and serve: Taste for seasoning and add salt and pepper if needed. Garnish with parsley and serve. Pair with a cabernet sauvignon, merlot, or zinfandel.

Twice Baked Potatoes

Ingredients

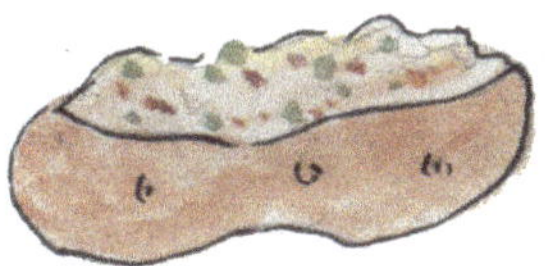

4 large baking potatoes
8 slices bacon
1 cup sour cream
½ cup milk
4 tablespoons butter
½ teaspoon salt
½ teaspoon pepper
1 cup shredded cheddar cheese, divided
8 green onions, sliced, divided

Directions

Gather ingredients and preheat the oven to 350°.

Bake potatoes in the preheated oven until tender, about 1 hour, depending on the size of your potatoes. Set potatoes aside until cool enough to handle.

Meanwhile, place bacon in a large, deep skillet. Cook over medium-high heat until evenly brown. Drain, crumble, and set aside.

Slice cooked potatoes in half lengthwise and scoop the flesh into a large bowl; save skins.

Add sour cream, milk, butter, salt, pepper, ½ cup cheese, and ½ of the green onions to the potato; mix with a hand mixer until well blended and creamy.

Spoon the mixture into the potato skins; top each with remaining cheese, green onions, and bacon.

Return potatoes to the preheated oven and continue baking until the cheese is melted, about 15 minutes. Serve Hot!

Angus conducted a thorough inspection of my home security, but his ultimate conclusion has left me unsettled, to say the least. After viewing the security footage from my outdoor camera and finding nothing, he claims it was an inside job! Now family and friends are all suspects, which leaves me feeling hurt and betrayed even though I suspected as much. I will need time to reflect on this before I decide how to handle such a delicate situation.

Eleanor's Super Secret Barbecue Sauce

Ingredients

8 oz. tomato sauce
1 cup ketchup
⅔ cup light brown sugar
¼ cup unsulphured molasses
⅔ cup red wine vinegar
2 teaspoons hickory flavored liquid smoke
½ teaspoon smoked paprika or regular paprika
½ teaspoon salt
¼ teaspoon onion powder
¼ teaspoon garlic powder
¼ teaspoon cayenne pepper
¼ teaspoon freshly ground black pepper
⅛ teaspoon chili powder
⅛ teaspoon ground mustard
⅛ teaspoon ground cinnamon
⅛ teaspoon ground black pepper

Directions

Add all ingredients to a large saucepan and mix together until smooth. Cook over medium heat, stirring frequently, until mixture comes to a boil, then reduce the heat and simmer for at least 20 minutes or up to one hour, stirring occasionally.

Remove from heat and allow to cool. The sauce will thicken slightly as it cools. Store in an air tight container in the fridge for up to three weeks.

Grilled Baby Back Ribs

Ingredients

1 tablespoon ground cumin
1 tablespoon chili powder
1 tablespoon paprika
salt and pepper to taste
3 pounds baby back pork ribs
1 cup of Eleanor's secret barbeque sauce

Directions

Preheat a gas grill for high heat, or arrange charcoal briquettes on one side of the barbeque. Lightly oil the grate.

Combine cumin, chili powder, paprika, salt, and pepper in a small jar; close the lid and shake to mix.

Trim the membrane sheath from the back of each rack. Run a small, sharp knife between the membrane and each rib, and snip off the membrane as much as possible. Sprinkle as much of the rub onto both sides of ribs as desired. To prevent ribs from becoming too dark and spicy, do not thoroughly rub spices into ribs. Store any unused spice mix in a jar for future use.

Place aluminum foil on the lower rack to capture drippings and prevent flare-ups. Lay ribs on the top rack of the grill (away from the coals, if you're using briquettes). Reduce gas heat to low and close the lid; cook ribs, undisturbed as possible, until meat pulls away easily from the bone, about 1 hour. An instant-read thermometer inserted into the center should read 145 degrees F (63° C).

Brush ribs with barbecue sauce, and grill for an additional 5 minutes. Serve ribs as a whole rack, or cut between each rib bone and pile individually on a platter. Serve with lots of napkins. Pair with a Bordeaux.

Crispy Yams or Sweet Potatoes

Ingredients

½ tablespoon coarse kosher salt
½ tablespoon ground black pepper
½ tablespoon light brown sugar
½ teaspoon chili powder
1 teaspoon paprika
1 teaspoon garlic powder
3 large sweet potatoes, cut into ½-inch cubes
3 tablespoons olive oil

Directions

Preheat oven to 450°. In a small bowl, mix together the salt, pepper, brown sugar, chili powder, paprika, and garlic powder.

Toss the sweet potatoes in olive oil, then add seasoning and toss to coat evenly. Place the seasoned sweet potatoes on a baking sheet lined with parchment paper with about a half-inch in between each one. Roast for 15 minutes, toss and continue roasting for 10–15 minutes until golden brown and crispy.

Coleslaw

Ingredients

Dressing
½ cup mayonnaise
2 tablespoons apple cider vinegar or fresh lemon juice
1 tablespoon sugar
1 tablespoon grainy mustard (optional)
½ teaspoon salt
½ teaspoon celery seed
½ teaspoon black pepper

Slaw
4 cups cabbage shredded
2 tart apples cored julienned (or shredded)
1 cup carrots shredded

Directions

Combine dressing ingredients in a small bowl and toss with slaw ingredients. Allow to sit for at least 1 hour before serving

Grilled Salmon with Beet and Orange Relish

Ingredients

Beet Orange Relish
2 yellow beets, boiled and peeled and diced
2 purple beets, boiled and peeled and diced
1 blood orange, the skin and pith cut off and diced
½ cup red onion, diced
2 tablespoons olive oil
2 tablespoons red wine vinegar
¼ cup orange juice
½ cup fresh parsley leaves
kosher salt

Grilled Salmon
2 eight-ounce Salmon filets with skin
2 tablespoons olive oil
kosher salt
Balsamic glaze (optional, for garnish)

Directions

Preheat a grill to high heat. While the grill is warming up, make the beet relish. In a medium bowl combine the beets, blood orange, onion, oil, vinegar, and orange juice and mix well. Season to taste with kosher salt and then toss in the fresh parsley leaves.

Rub the salmon generously with olive oil and sprinkle with kosher salt. Turn the heat to medium on the barbeque (this can also be done on a grilling pan on the stovetop) and then place the skin side down. Cook for 3 minutes and then flip and cook for 1–2 more. The fish should be barely cooked through.

Transfer the salmon to a serving platter and serve immediately topped with the beet orange relish.

Preparation time: 20 minute(s)

Cooking time: 6 minute(s)

Number of servings: 2

Pair this dish with a pinot noir or a pinot gris if you prefer white.

Imagine my surprise when I began to prepare dinner and found my secret recipes were once again on the shelf where they belong! It was painfully clear that a family member had taken the recipes, but who and why …

After much thought I have decided to invite my daughters and their families to dinner and present them with the evidence and determine their guilt by their reactions and maybe even get a confession. It would never do to accuse my coffee friends. I'm certain they would be horrified.

Lime Kristina Cocktail

Fill a rocks glass with ice. Add equal parts gin and sweetened lime juice. Fill glass with sparkling water. Mix and serve. Garnish with a slice of lime.

Eleanor's Confession Recipe

Ingredients

Tequila shots
Beer or other long drink (such as a Lime Kristina)

Directions

Ply guests with shots of tequila and beer while playing Yahtzee.

The cursed ace: Whenever a player rolls an ace, they drink. And yes, if they roll four aces in one turn, they have to drink four times, and so and so on.

Yahtzee: Every time a player rolls a Yahtzee, they can assign the other players to drink. They can divide the rolled numbers between the players. For example, one player rolls a Yahtzee with the number 4, then they can assign four people to drink.

The picky one: The picky one is simple but cruel: Every time a player decides to reroll every dice, they have to finish their drink.

The 100 points: If one player rolls a Yahtzee for the second time or more, they drink a shot.

The waterfall: Whenever a player rolls a small or large straight, this player starts a waterfall. This player starts drinking in one go and the other players have to follow him in line. All players have to drink until the player before them stops drinking.

Strangely enough when I explained the game to my family, they became immediately suspicious and accused me of trying to get them drunk. Amy and Erin began to babble and confessed to taking the recipes without drinking a drop (it's obviously a very effective technique). They then presented me with a beautiful cookbook filled with their favorite recipes (published and edited by my publishers) and explained their only motive was to make a few copies for family only so that the recipes could be passed down through the generations as a tribute to me. How could I be angry?

Of course, my publishers felt little guilt regarding the sanctity of my secrets and put this little cookbook out into the world.

Recipe for Feeling Your Best

- Eat nutritiously
- Move dynamically
- Go outside for light and fresh air
- Rest well. Get plenty of sleep
- Look for the positive by asking what you are thankful for, what you are excited about, and what you can do to make someone else feel good.

- **Choose to be happy!**

Catch up with Eleanor Penrose and all the colorful characters in the Coastal Coffee Club Mysteries Series, featuring:

Purchase at:

GladEye Press
www.gladeyepress.com